WITHDRAWN

W9-ALM-134

For Lucia, ever onwards

ABOUT THIS BOOK

The illustrations for this book were done in watercolor, gouache, and colored pencil on both Fabiano 140lb hot-pressed and Arches 140lb cold-pressed papers. This book was edited by Susan Rich and designed by Saho Fujii. The production was supervised by Patricia Alvarado, and the production editor was Annie McDonnell. The text was set in Mrs Eaves, and the display type is Mrs Eaves.

Copyright © 2021 by David Soman • Cover illustration copyright © 2021 by David Soman. • Cover design by Saho Fujii. • Cover copyright © 2021 by Hachette Book Group, Inc. • Hachette Book Group supports the right to free expression and the value of copyright. The purpose of copyright is to encourage writers and artists to produce the creative works that enrich our culture. • The scanning, uploading, and distribution of this book without permission is a theft of the author's intellectual property. If you would like permission to use material from the book (other than for review purposes), please contact permissions@hbgusa.com. Thank you for your support of the author's rights. • Little, Brown and Company • Hachette Book Group • 1290 Avenue of the Americas, New York, NY 10104 • Visit us at LBYR.com • First Edition: November 2021 • Little, Brown and Company is a division of Hachette Book Group, Inc. • The Little, Brown name and logo are trademarks of Hachette Book Group, Inc. • The publisher is not responsible for websites (or their content) that are not owned by the publisher. • Library of Congress Cataloging-in-Publication Data • Names: Soman, David, author, illustrator. • Title: The impossible mountain / by David Soman. • Description: First edition. | New York : Little, Brown and Company, 2021. | Audience: Ages 3–6. | Summary: Anna and Finn look over the wall that surrounds their tiny village and discover a mountain, which the villagers warn cannot be climbed, but the siblings are determined to reach the top. • Identifiers: LCCN 2020050443 | ISBN 9780316427746 (hardcover) • Subjects: CYAC: Determination (Personality trait)—Fiction. | Persistence—Fiction. | Mountaineering—Fiction. | Brothers and sisters—Fiction. • Classification: LCC PZ7.S696224 Imp 2021 | DDC [E]—dc23 • LC record available at https://lccn.loc.gov/2020050443 • ISBN 978-0-316-42774-6 • PRINTED IN CHINA • APS • 10 9 8 7 6 5 4 3 2 1

The Impossible
MOUNTAIN

DAVID SOMAN

LB

Little, Brown and Company

New York Boston

In a village sheltered by a high, heavy wall, Anna grew up,
like a wildflower between the stones.

She and her little brother, Finn, had always been told that the Wall kept them safe from a scary, unknown world.

So, Anna and Finn spent their days exploring the Village,
but the world was small inside a circle of stone.

Then, one day, they climbed the Wall.

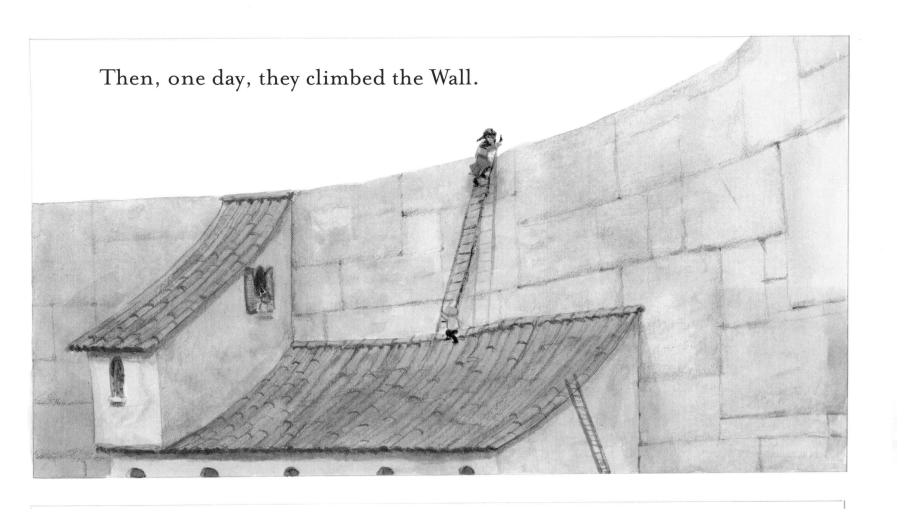

From there, they could see, spread below, the whole
Village, bigger than they could stretch their arms.
But when they turned around…

"Wow," said Anna.
"Wow," said Finn.

After that, the Mountain was always in Anna's thoughts,
a song she couldn't stop hearing. As time passed, the song
grew stronger and clearer. It was a song about the world
outside the village walls, a song about the Mountain, a
song about what might lie beyond it.

Anna heard it, and then she knew, plainly knew, she
had to climb the Mountain. She had to see the world.

And so, she thought, should Finn.

As she packed for the journey, she told Finn, "You're coming with me."

"Where?" he asked.

"To climb the Mountain," answered Anna.

"To the top?" he asked, excited.

"To the top," she said.

So, Finn packed, too.

As they walked to the village gate, a crowd gathered.

The blacksmith said, "Climbing the Mountain is impossible; you'll never get past the River!"

"I can," said Anna.

"The Mountain is too big," said a mean boy. "You're not brave enough to climb the Cliffs!"

"I am," said Anna.

"And don't forget about the Great and Terrible Bear!" called the Baker.

"I'm not scared," said Anna.

"Me neither!" said Finn, and together they walked past the crowd and through the gate.

Soon they felt as if they had been swallowed by the Woods.

There was no path, but as long as they were going up,
it seemed like the right way to go.

They heard the Falls before
they saw them.

The River thundered and
poured past them, beautiful
and frightening.

They couldn't cross here,
thought Anna, but if they
followed along the bank...

The stones stood in the water
like a parade of turtles.
"If we hopped…," said Anna.
"I'm a good hopper," said Finn.
"Let's go, then," said Anna.

The stones were wet and slippery, and
the last one was far from the shore.
"I'm not sure…," said Finn.
"I'll catch you," called Anna.
And she did.

Thrilled, and a little relieved,
they took a break by the water.

Moving like smoke between the trees,
the Wolves surprised them. No one had
said anything about Wolves.

"I'll protect you," said Finn.

"Not like that, Finn," said Anna,
frightened, "like this."

BRAMMP BAH BAH BRAMMP!!!

The Wolves fled back into the Woods.

The Woods behind them,
they came upon a wild orchard,
shining, buzzing with bees and butterflies.
　"Apples!" cried Finn.
　"Apples," agreed Anna, eating some and
collecting more for later.

The climb grew harder and Anna was never
entirely sure of the way.
Sometimes the Mountain seemed to show them…

...sometimes it did not.

"I can't climb this," said Anna.

"Me neither," said Finn, looking over his shoulder. "Should we go back?"

"No!" said Anna. "There must be some way…"

BAAAH!

The Mountain Goat seemed to be standing on the cliff's face, impossible. But then Anna saw the trail, so thin it looked like it was scratched into the Mountain's side.

"This is the way, Finn!" she cried.

Carefully, they inched along to the sound of the
small pebbles they dislodged bouncing down, lost below.

"Thank you, Mr. Goat!" called Finn as it bounded away.

"This must be the top!"

But it wasn't.

Finn looked at Anna, a question.

"Let's keep going,"

said Anna.

When the snow began, the flakes spun in the air. Soon it became hard to see, and then hard to walk.

Anna was getting very tired and cold, when, through the snow, she saw a slight darkness ahead of them. A cave!

Shivering, Anna built a little fire and made them cups of tea. It was only then that she saw they weren't alone.

"Anna," whispered Finn. "It's the Great and Terrible Bear."

With shaking hands, Anna offered him an apple she had saved. The Bear sniffed it, and in one motion, it was gone.

Then the Bear circled them, lay down, a large, cozy curve,
and before long, was asleep. And soon, so were Anna and Finn.

When the Sun peeked through the entrance,
they all awoke. The snow had piled up,
almost covering the cave's mouth.

Giving a shake, the Bear plowed easily through it, like a ship
through the sea, and led Anna and Finn through the field of snow.

Small against the huge spine of the Mountain,
they climbed on.
"I think we're near the top!" said Anna.

But they weren't. There was more, always more.
Anna stared. Maybe the Mountain was too big, maybe
the villagers had been right, maybe she couldn't get to
the top, maybe it was impossible. Maybe?

Anna looked at Finn. He smiled
at her, an answer.
"To the top," said Anna.
"To the top!" cheered Finn.

And then at the next rise, like a gift, Anna looked down
and saw her village far, far below. It was so small she felt
she could hold the whole thing in her cupped hands. She
thought she could even see the villagers, tiny moving dots,
going about their day.

Together, they climbed up through the swirling clouds,
to the Top of the Mountain.

"Anna, look!" said Finn.

The world was full of mountains,
all of them waiting to be climbed.